THE
CLASSIC TREASURY
OF

PRINCESS
FAIRY TALES

Illustrated by

Peter Malone

Retold by

Margaret Clark

COURAGE
BOOKS
AN IMPRINT OF RUNNING PRESS
PHILADELPHIA • LONDON

9 8 7 6 5 4 3 2 1
Digit on the right indicates the number of this printing

Library of Congress Control Number: 2005923031

ISBN-13: 978-0-7624-3162-5
ISBN-10: 0-7624-3162-8

Designed by Frances J. Soo Ping Chow
Edited by Susan K. Hom
Typography: Centaur MT, ITC Berkeley, and Schneidler Initials

This book may be ordered by mail from the publisher.
But try your bookstore first!

Published by Courage Books, an imprint of
Running Press Book Publishers
2300 Chestnut Street
Philadelphia, Pennsylvania 19103-4371

Visit us on the web!
www.runningpress.com

CONTENTS

Introduction

7

Cinderella

8

Snow White and the Seven Dwarfs

14

The Frog Prince

23

The Sleeping Beauty

27

The Twelve Dancing Princesses

33

Rumpelstiltskin

39

The Princess and the Pea

44

Beauty and the Beast

47

INTRODUCTION

EVERYONE KNOWS THAT CINDERELLA went to the ball and lost her slipper as she hurried away to be home by midnight. But who remembers how kind she was to the stepsisters who teased and bullied her from morning till night? It was her sweet nature, reflected in her lovely face, that won the heart of the prince.

Beauty was the youngest of her father's children, but she was the most loving and the bravest. She took her father's place at once when the Beast threatened to kill him for stealing a rose. With great courage, she looked into the eyes of the Beast as they talked together every night. She saw the beautiful soul behind his terrifying appearance.

The miller's daughter was clever—much more intelligent than her father, whose boast that she could spin straw into gold caused her so much trouble. But she used her good sense and kept her nerve, so Rumpelstiltskin lost his claim to her baby daughter.

Snow White never gave a thought to her own beauty. She could not understand her stepmother's jealousy. So when the seven dwarfs gave her shelter, she diligently helped them with their household chores. And after she married her prince, she never forgot them.

In every fairy tale in this collection, you will find a girl who is kind and brave, who works hard and enjoys using her brain, and who, in fact, possesses all the virtues of a true princess.

CINDERELLA

ONCE THERE WAS A GIRL whose mother had taught her always to be kind. "If you are kind to other people," her mother said, "then they will be kind to you."

But when the girl was still young, her mother died, and soon afterward her father married again. The girl's stepmother was not kind to her, nor were her two stepsisters. The girl began to wonder whether her mother had been right, but she was naturally sweet-natured so she did not complain.

The girl's stepmother made her sleep in the attic on an old mattress that was hard and lumpy, while her stepsisters took over her bedroom. They were given two large looking-glasses in which they gazed at themselves during every hour of the day. The girl was told to do the worst of the housework. When she had finished at the end of the day, she would go into the kitchen and sit among the cinders that fell from the fire. That's why the older stepsister gave her the nickname Cinderbottom, but the younger one thought this was rude. Feeling sorry for the girl, she changed it to Cinderella.

One day, the stepsisters were invited by the prince to a ball. They were so excited that for the next few days they could think about nothing but what they would wear.

"Cinderella!" called the elder sister. "Tell me how beautiful I shall look in this red velvet!"

"It's lovely," answered Cinderella, thinking to herself that perhaps red was not the best color for someone so fat.

"Come over here," said the younger sister. "Look at the gold on my cape! You will have to iron it very carefully. This is the first ball I've ever been to. Wouldn't you like to be coming too, Cinderella?"

Cinderella wanted to cry with envy but she only replied sadly, "Don't tease me, please."

The sisters laughed. "No, we won't tease you—but how could Cinderbottom possibly go to the ball? She has to stay at home, sitting in the cinders."

Cinderella helped them put on the red velvet and the gold cape. She watched as they set off for the royal palace. Then she sat down in the cinders and cried and cried.

Out of nowhere appeared a woman who said she was Cinderella's fairy godmother. She told Cinderella to stop crying. Then the fairy godmother asked her what was the matter.

"I wish I could . . . I wish I could . . ." sobbed Cinderella.

"Go to the ball?" asked her godmother.

Cinderella nodded.

"Then we have a lot to do," said her godmother briskly. "Bring me a pumpkin from the garden."

Cinderella began to cheer up. She brought in the biggest pumpkin she could find. Her godmother took a kitchen knife, hollowed out the pumpkin, and made three small holes in each side of it. She touched it with her wand, and there stood a golden coach!

Cinderella was spellbound. "Hurry up and look in the mousetrap," said her godmother. As Cinderella let out six gray mice, her godmother touched each one with her wand—and there, between the shafts of the golden coach, stood six gray horses!

"Let me look in the rat trap," said Cinderella. And her godmother changed a big, whiskered rat into a large, handsome coachman.

Then Cinderella was sent into the garden again to chase six lizards. In a moment, they were footmen. One stood by the door of the golden coach, holding it open.

"How can I go to the ball in these ragged clothes?" asked Cinderella. Instantly the rags became a ball dress of gold and silver silk. On her feet were two elegant glass slippers.

"Now, off to the ball!" said her godmother. "But remember, you must be home by midnight. When the clock strikes twelve, your coach will turn back into a pumpkin,

your horses into mice, your coachman into a rat, your footmen into lizards, and your clothes into rags."

When Cinderella arrived at the ball, everyone stopped dancing to look at her. The musicians put down their instruments. No one had seen such a beauty before. They all peered at every detail of her dress and the ribbons in her hair. The prince stepped forward to lead her into the room where a banquet was to be served.

No one knew who the girl was. Her stepsisters did not recognize her—even when she sat down beside them and offered them oranges and lemons, which the prince had given her.

When Cinderella heard the clock strike a quarter to twelve, she remembered what her godmother had said. She hurried home, where her clothes turned to rags again. She was just in time to open the front door for her stepsisters.

"Oh, what a wonderful time we had," they said. "We met a beautiful princess. She was so kind to us and gave us oranges and lemons. The prince wants to know who she is, but no one can tell him."

Cinderella smiled to herself. The next day the prince gave another ball, and again he spent the whole evening at Cinderella's side. She was having such a delightful evening that she forgot what time it was. As the clock began to strike twelve, she rushed down the stairs, losing one of her glass slippers. The other was still on her foot when she reached home, but her dress, the coach, the horses, the coachman, and the footmen had all disappeared.

A few days later, a messenger from the prince came to announce that he had a glass slipper. If it was a perfect fit, then the prince would marry the maiden. The stepsisters began to try it. They both had rather large feet, so the slipper was much too small for them. Cinderella, who had of course recognized it, asked quietly to put it on. The stepsisters jeered. When it fit and Cinderella produced the second slipper, they realized who she was. At that moment, her fairy godmother appeared and turned her rags into an even finer dress than she had worn before. The stepsisters were ashamed and pleaded with Cinderella to forgive them for all the unkindness they had shown her.

Of course Cinderella forgave them and the three all went to the palace. On the day that Cinderella married her prince, the stepsisters were married to two noblemen of his court. And Cinderella never forgot what her mother had taught her.

SNOW WHITE
AND THE SEVEN DWARFS

A QUEEN ONCE SAT AT HER WINDOW, looking out at the snow falling from a gray sky. While she was sewing, her needle suddenly slipped and pricked her finger and three spots of blood dropped on to her work. The queen was startled, but she saw this as a good omen and made a wish. "May my baby daughter be white as the snow, red as my blood, and black as the ebony frame of this window."

When the baby was born shortly thereafter, her skin was white as snow, her cheeks red as blood, and her hair black as ebony. The king and queen named her Snow White because she was born in winter.

Unfortunately the queen did not live to see her daughter grow up, and the king soon married again. His second wife was more beautiful than the first, but she was extremely vain. She loved looking at herself, especially in an enchanted looking glass that spoke. She would go to it and say:

"Looking glass, tell me once again

How fair my face and fine my hair,

Where is there anyone to compare?"

And the looking glass always answered, "There's none so fair as you, my queen."

But baby Snow White grew lovelier every day. By the time she was seven, she was prettier than her stepmother.

So when the queen went to the looking glass one day, it gave a new reply to her question. It said:

"You are fair as ever, my queen,

But Snow White is fairest of all we've seen."

The queen was so angry when she heard this that she ordered a servant to take Snow White into the forest and leave her to die. The servant did this with a heavy heart.

Snow White was frightened by the darkness under the trees and the wild animals that she could hear all round her. She walked as far as she could, looking for a way out of the forest. At nightfall she came to a cottage. She knocked on the door, but there was no answer so she went inside. A table was laid with seven places, and along the wall were seven beds. She was very hungry by now, so she took a tiny piece of bread from each of the seven plates and drank a tiny sip of wine from each of the seven glasses. Then she lay down on each of the seven beds. The last proved the most comfortable, so she curled up and went to sleep.

She was still fast asleep when the seven dwarfs who lived in the cottage returned home from the mountains where they worked at mining gold. They lit their seven lanterns and saw that someone had come into their house.

"Who has been nibbling my bread?" asked one.

"Who has been drinking from my glass?" asked another.

Then they all looked at their beds and asked together, "Who's been lying on my bed?"

The seventh dwarf called the others to look at the lovely little girl asleep on his bed. They were all so pleased to see her that they ate their supper very quietly, so as not to wake her. The seventh dwarf spent the night resting on each of the other beds in turn, so that the little girl was not disturbed.

The next morning Snow White told the seven dwarfs what had happened to her. The dwarfs felt very sorry for her and they said she could stay as long as she liked. Perhaps, they thought, she would do the cooking and a bit of housework for them. They warned Snow White to be very careful while they were out at work because they were sure the queen would come looking for her.

The queen was certain that Snow White must be dead by now, so she went to her looking glass and said:

"Looking glass, tell me once again
How fair my face and fine my hair,

Where is there anyone to compare?"

And the looking glass answered:

"Here is none so fair as you, my queen.

But where seven dwarfs live over the hill

There Snow White keeps their house and still

She is more fair than you, my queen."

The queen was much alarmed because she knew the looking glass never lied. She put on the disguise of a peddler and walked over the hill to the dwarfs' cottage. "Come and see what I have to sell!" she cried. "Ribbons, lace, buttons, and thread!" Snow White opened the door and did not recognize her stepmother, the queen.

"Oh, what a pretty child!" said the wicked queen. "You need a new sash for your dress. I'll tie it for you." She put the sash around Snow White's waist and pulled it so tight that Snow White fainted and fell to the ground. "Good riddance," said the queen.

When the seven dwarfs came home, Snow White was still lying on the ground. They untied the sash, and slowly she felt better again. The dwarfs said, "You really must be careful. Don't open the door to anyone while we are out."

As soon as the queen was back at her palace, she went to her looking glass and asked her usual question. To her fury, it answered:

"Here is none so fair as you, my queen.

But where seven dwarfs live over the hill

There Snow White keeps their house and still

She is more fair than you, my queen."

The queen was more angry than ever before. The next day she disguised herself again and put some deadly poison on a comb. She walked over the hill to the dwarfs' cottage. "Come and see what I have to sell!" she cried. "Combs for your lovely black hair!"

But Snow White said, "I must not open the door."

So the queen went to the window of the cottage and held up her tray of combs. And Snow White leaned out and picked up the prettiest comb, which was the poisoned one and put it in her hair. As soon as the comb touched her head, she collapsed to the ground. "Good riddance," said the queen.

When the dwarfs came home from work, Snow White was still lying on the ground. They took away the comb, and slowly Snow White felt better again. She told the dwarfs exactly what had happened. They warned her not to be deceived by the queen any more.

The queen meanwhile went to her looking glass. When she asked the usual question, it gave her the same reply. She became hysterical with rage. "I shall kill Snow White, even if it means killing myself as well," she shrieked.

She thought very hard about how she could do this. She found an apple with a rosy skin, which she pierced with a pin and poisoned. Then she put on another disguise and walked over the hill to the dwarfs' cottage. "Come to the window, sweetheart," she shouted. "Come see what a beautiful present that I've brought you."

Snow White came to the window and said, "The dwarfs say I should trust no one."

The queen laughed and said, "You can trust me. I'll eat half of this apple. You can have the other half. Then you'll know that it isn't poisoned."

So the queen bit into the apple, knowing which side held the poison. She gave the rest to Snow White. As soon as a piece of the apple was in Snow White's mouth, she fell down as if dead.

"This time, good riddance forever!" said the queen, who went home quickly to talk to her looking glass. She asked it the usual question.

It answered, "There's none so fair as you, my queen!"

Then the queen was happy at last. But the seven dwarfs were very sad when they came home and found Snow White on the ground. For three days they watched her, sprinkling her face with water and saying her name over and over again. She never moved, so they decided that she must be dead. Yet she looked so lovely—just as she had when alive—so they did not want to bury her body in the cold earth. Instead they put her in a glass coffin with her name written on it in gold.

The dwarfs put the coffin on a hillside, where one of them always kept vigil beside it. The birds, who had loved Snow White, also kept watch over her—an owl, a raven, and a dove.

Snow White lay in her coffin for a long time but she remained as beautiful as before. A prince, passing by, saw her and instantly fell in love with her. The dwarfs did not want to part with her, but the prince persuaded them to let him take her body back to his kingdom. As he lifted the coffin, the piece of apple fell out of Snow White's mouth, and she opened her eyes. "Who are you?" she asked and the prince told her everything that had happened and how he knew he would always love her.

Snow White agreed to go with him. By the time they reached his palace, she was as much in love with him as he with her.

Their wedding was celebrated with a feast, to which everyone in the neighboring kingdoms was invited, including Snow White's stepmother. As the queen put on her best clothes, she said to her looking glass:

"Looking glass, tell me once again

How fair my face and fine my hair,

Where is there anyone to compare?"

And the looking glass answered:

"Here is none so fair as you, my queen,

But fairer still is the prince's bride."

The queen could hardly believe her ears, but she went to the feast. When she saw that the prince's bride was Snow White, she choked with envy and died on the spot.

The prince and Snow White lived happily together. When the prince's father died, they became king and queen of his kingdom. But they did not forget the seven dwarfs who had saved Snow White. They often visited the cottage over the hill.

THE FROG PRINCE

THERE WAS ONCE A PRINCESS who loved to walk through the woods by herself, playing with a golden ball that was her favorite toy. She would throw it in the air and run to catch it before it touched the ground.

One day, she threw the ball so high that it fell a long way off. She followed it as it rolled away among the trees, until she heard a splash as it landed in the water of a deep spring. She looked into the water but she could not see it.

She sat down sadly on the bank and began to cry. "Oh, if only I could get my ball back! I would give all of my clothes, even my jewels, just to play with it again."

At that moment, a frog's head appeared above the water. "Dear princess," said the frog, "why are you crying?"

"Because I've lost my ball in the spring," replied the princess. "And what can you do about it, you slimy thing?"

"I can find it for you," said the frog. "But if I do, you must promise to love me and let me share what you eat off your golden plate. And you must let me sleep on your bed."

The princess thought that this was a very silly thing for the frog to say. She knew he couldn't even get out of the water, never mind make his way to her palace. The princess wanted her golden ball so much that she agreed to give him what he asked. Then he quickly put his head under water and dived to the bottom of the spring. He returned with the ball in his mouth and threw it on to the bank.

The princess picked up her ball and ran away from the spring, never thinking of the frog nor hearing him say, "Wait for me, princess. You promised!"

She played with her ball all day. When evening came, she sat down to dinner with her father. Before they had started to eat, the princess heard a strange noise—plop, plop—as if something were coming up the marble stairs outside. Then there was a knock at the door. A voice said:

"Open the door, my princess dear,

Open the door, for your true love is here!

Remember the promise you made to me

When we met by the spring near the greenwood tree."

The princess opened the door. There was the frog, whom she had forgotten. She shivered with fright and shut the door.

"Whatever is the matter?" asked the king.

"There is a slimy frog sitting outside the door," said the princess. "He got my ball out of the spring this morning. I told him he could share what I eat off my golden plate and sleep on my bed—but I didn't think he could get out of the water. And now he is here and wants to come in."

There was another knock at the door and a voice repeated:

"Open the door, my princess dear,

Open the door, for your true love is here!

Remember the promise you made to me

When we met by the spring near the greenwood tree."

The king looked at his daughter and said, sadly, "If you made a promise, then you have to keep it."

So the princess opened the door and the frog came in. Plop, plop, he hopped to the princess's place at the table. "Please put me on a chair by your side," he said. Next he asked her to move her golden plate, so that he could share her dinner.

When he had eaten his fill, the frog said, "I am so tired. Please take me upstairs and put me on your bed."

He slept on a pillow until dawn came. Then he jumped on to the floor and hopped all the way out of the palace.

The princess was glad that he had gone and believed that she would never see him again. But she was wrong. That night he knocked again on her door. She heard again his plaintive voice:

"Open the door, my princess dear,

Open the door, for your true love is here!

Remember the promise you made to me

When we met by the spring near the greenwood tree."

So she let him in. Once more, he slept on a pillow on her bed. The third night, all happened as before.

But on the third morning she woke to find that the frog had disappeared. At the foot of her bed, standing so still and gazing at her, was a young man. "Where have you come from?" she asked.

"I am the frog who frightened you," he said. "I am so sorry, but I was under a spell put on me by a fairy who did not like me. I knew the spell could only be broken if I found a princess who would let me share what she ate off her golden plate and sleep on her bed for three nights. And I had the good fortune to find you! If you will now come with me to my father's kingdom we can be married and love each other for as long as we live."

And that is what they did.

THE SLEEPING BEAUTY

THERE ONCE LIVED A KING and queen who had everything anyone could wish for—a fine palace with more rooms than they could count, a park full of trees and flowers, stables full of horses, and plenty of money. Yet they were very unhappy, because the only thing they really wanted was a child.

One day, as the queen wandered through the park, she came upon a fish lying on the bank of a stream. It was almost dead, so the queen picked it up and laid it gently in the water. The fish lifted its head and said, "How kind you are! You have given me what I wanted, the chance to swim home, so now you will have what you want—a baby daughter."

When the baby girl was born, the king and queen were so happy that they decided to share their great joy with everyone in the kingdom by giving a feast in the palace. The king sent out invitations to everyone he knew and many of his citizens he hadn't met before. Then the queen said he must invite the fairies, because they would be sure to bring presents for the new princess.

All the tables were set for the feast with golden plates, knives, forks, and spoons decorated with rubies and diamonds, but the servants found they were one plate short. So the king invited only twelve of the thirteen fairies in his kingdom, hoping that the one who had not been seen for many years would never find out.

After all the food had been eaten, and all the wine drunk, the fairies brought their gifts to the princess's cradle. The fairy gifts included talents of all kinds. They promised that she would grow up to be wise and beautiful, to sing like a nightingale, and to dance as lightly as they did. Just as the twelfth fairy was about to speak, there was a crash, as the doors of the hall burst open. In came the thirteenth fairy, her face red with rage. She

shouted at the king that she would have her revenge for being the only person in the land not invited to the feast.

"You will be sorry!" she screamed. "When your precious daughter is fifteen, she will prick her finger on a spindle, and she will die!"

Then all the guests cried out, "Oh no!" and began to weep and wail. But they had forgotten the twelfth fairy, who had not yet spoken.

"Don't be afraid," she said. "I cannot undo the spell completely, but when the princess pricks her finger she will not die. She will fall asleep for one hundred years and then a prince will wake her."

The king was determined that his daughter should never prick her finger on a spindle. He gave an order that henceforth no one would be allowed to spin wool or thread ever again. All the spindles and spinning wheels in his kingdom were thrown onto an enormous bonfire and destroyed. Then he and the queen sighed with relief.

The princess grew up to be wise and beautiful, as the fairies had promised. She could sing like a nightingale and dance as lightly as they did.

On the morning of her fifteenth birthday, the princess was alone in the palace, while her parents were visiting a neighbor. The princess was restless. She wandered around the rooms that no one had ever bothered to count, until she came to a stone staircase. She ran up the steps and, opening a little door with a golden key, found an old woman sitting by a wheel, with a sharp, pointed stick in her hand.

"What are you doing?" the princess asked.

"Why, I'm spinning," said the old woman. "Haven't you ever seen a spinning wheel before?"

"No, but I'd love to try it," answered the princess. And she took the spindle from the old woman. Just as the fairy had foretold, she pricked her finger. With a cry, the princess fell to the floor.

The old woman was very frightened. She knew nothing of the princess nor of the fairy's curse nor of the king's order that all spindles should be burned. The old woman had not been out of her tower for many years. Now she ran down the steps shouting for help.

The king, who had by now returned, saw his daughter and remembered what the twelfth fairy had said. He had his daughter carried to her own bed, her face as beautiful as ever and her body still warm—for she was not dead, but in a deep sleep.

And when the king left her room, he began to yawn, and the queen, too. They both went to sleep in their chairs. Soon everyone else in the palace slept—including the horses in the stables and the watchdogs at the doors. The princess's puppy, who lay beside her on her bed, was soon asleep as well. Even the clocks in the palace stopped. For a long time, nothing moved inside the enchanted palace.

Outside, in the park, the trees and thorny bushes went untended and grew so thick that only the tallest towers of the palace could be seen.

After one hundred years, the son of the king of a neighboring country came by and, seeing the towers, asked who lived there. A peasant, who was very old, remembered a story that his father had told him about a lovely princess who would sleep for a hundred years and could only be awakened by a prince.

The prince was very excited by this news and started to push his way into the thicket. To his surprise, the trees bent their branches and the thorny brambles moved aside so that he could pass easily between them. When he came to the palace, he saw the watchdogs at the doors and the horses in the stables, all still as if they were dead.

He stepped inside and found all the people there looking as unmoving as statues. Something drew him to the room where the princess lay on her bed with her puppy beside her. The prince thought he had never seen such a lovely face. He knelt down by the bed.

The princess opened her eyes and looked at him. "Are you a prince?" she asked. "What a long time you have been in coming!"

Then they talked about all that had happened and what the princess remembered. The puppy woke up and wanted to go outside. So they all walked together through the palace. In every room, the palace servants stretched themselves and resumed whatever they had been doing so long ago.

The prince and princess were married, just as soon as everything in the palace had been put to rights. The king and queen gave a wedding feast for them, but this time they made sure everyone was invited.

The Twelve Dancing Princesses

THERE WAS ONCE A KING who had twelve daughters. He loved them all, even though he sometimes wished he had a son. He loved them so much that he liked to know exactly where they all were at every minute of the day. When they went to bed, he locked the door of the biggest bedroom in his castle, where they slept in their twelve beds.

One morning, when their nurse went into the room to wake them, she found them looking pale and yawning, as if they had not slept at all. Then she looked at the shoes by every bed and she saw that the soles were worn through, as if the princesses had been dancing all night.

The same thing happened the next day and the next. When the king asked his daughters what they had been doing, they just said "Nothing." The king grew very angry and announced that if anyone found out where his daughters danced all night, that man could choose any one of them for his wife. But for the man who tried to do this and failed, after three nights the punishment would be death.

A prince from a nearby kingdom was the first to try. He sat by the door after the princesses had gone to bed. The prince thought how easy it was going to be to watch through the night. But his eyes closed and when he awoke it was morning. The princesses were still in their beds but their shoes were full of holes.

The next night, the prince tried so hard to stay awake, but the same thing happened. After the third night, he went to the king and said he had no idea where the princesses went, so the king had his head cut off.

This did not stop other princes coming, but none of them could solve the mystery.

So they all suffered the same fate.

Then an old soldier, returning from the wars, passed near the king's castle. An old woman sitting by the road spoke to him. "If you want to be the next king," she said, "why not try your luck? I'll help you. Take this cloak—it will make you invisible so that you can follow the princesses wherever they go. But when they bid you goodnight and give you a glass of wine, don't touch it. Just pretend to drink it and close your eyes."

So that's what the old soldier did. As soon as he had pretended to fall asleep, the princesses got out of their beds, laughing. They dressed themselves in their prettiest gowns and cloaks. They made quite a noise because they were so happy and excited— but the youngest was very quiet. "I feel something is wrong; I don't think we should go out tonight." But the others laughed even more. The eldest skipped to the top of her bed and clapped her hands twice.

Then the bed disappeared, and a trap door opened in the floor. One by one, the princesses stepped through the trap door. The soldier quickly put on the cloak that made him invisible and followed them. As he caught up with the last, who was the youngest, he trod on the hem of her dress. She cried out, "There's someone following us; I know something's wrong!" But the others laughed again, and the eldest said crossly, "Stop being so silly."

So down into the earth went the twelve princesses and the old soldier, and they came to a glade of trees with silver leaves that gleamed in the moonlight. The soldier, thinking he would need some proof for the king of where they had been, broke off a spray of leaves and the tree squeaked with pain.

"What was that?" asked the youngest princess. "Something is wrong. We never heard a noise like that before."

The eldest said, "There's nothing wrong. It's the princes who are waiting for us. They are shouting because they're excited."

At this, all the princesses started to skip and jump with happiness. The old soldier had a hard time keeping up with them, but as they passed more trees with leaves of gold and diamonds, he snapped off a branch of each. There were more squeaks from the

trees and the youngest princess was frightened, but the eldest told her again not to be so silly. "It's the princes, I told you. Do hurry!"

Suddenly they came out of the trees onto the shore of a lake. There on the water were twelve small boats and in each, a prince in dancing clothes, his hands already on the oars. Into the boats jumped the twelve princesses. The soldier squeezed himself into the same boat as the youngest. As they pulled away from the shore, the prince with the youngest princess said, "This boat seems very heavy tonight; I'm doing my best but I can't keep up with the others."

The youngest princess was trying not to be silly, so she said, "It must be the weather. It's very warm."

At the other end of the lake was a castle with towers and turrets, lit with thousands of candles. Men came to the water's edge to hold the boats while the princes and princesses stepped out and all ran together into the great ballroom. Each prince danced with his princess all night long, only stopping now and then to drink from golden

goblets of wine. But whenever the soldier in his invisible cloak saw a goblet set before one of the princesses, he emptied it before she could touch it. The youngest princess now knew there was something badly wrong but she could do nothing about it. The eldest told her for the third time not to be so silly.

When the princesses had worn out their shoes, they had to go home. So the princes rowed them across the lake. This time the soldier went in the boat with the eldest princess. Then they had to say goodbye. The youngest princess cried, but the others cheerfully waved to the princes, promising to be back the next night.

The soldier was careful to walk ahead of the princesses through the trees (they were by now very tired) so he managed to climb the steps first and lie down before they did. They heard his snoring before they got into their beds, and they thought their secret was quite safe.

The soldier said nothing about what he had seen until after the third night, when he brought back one of the golden goblets, hidden under his cloak.

At the end of the third day, the king summoned the soldier before the whole court to tell them where the princesses went to wear out their shoes dancing through the night. Then the soldier told all about the trap door and the steps that led to the glades of trees, whose leaves were made of silver and gold and diamonds. He told about the twelve princes who rowed the princesses across the lake to the castle, where they danced until the dawn of day. He showed the king the branches of the trees that he had brought from underground and the golden goblet from the castle.

The princesses were hiding behind the great doors to the courtroom and heard every word the soldier said. So when their father called for them and asked whether the soldier was telling the truth, they meekly bowed their heads and mumbled yes.

They knew then that the king would have to keep his word and let the soldier choose one of them for his wife. They looked at each other as the soldier listened to the king. The soldier answered, "I am not a young man, so I choose the eldest of your daughters."

The king decided that the wedding should take place at once, before another night passed. No one knows whether the princesses ever danced in the underground castle again.

RUMPELSTILTSKIN

THERE WAS ONCE A MILLER who had a very clever daughter. She could look after the mill that ground his flour. She could work out how much he should charge the customers who bought his flour. The miller's daughter could spin the finest wool and make clothes for him and herself. She was also very beautiful.

The miller was so proud of her that he often talked about her. One day, when the king passed by and saw the girl, he asked her father who she was. "Why," said the miller, "that's my daughter. She does so much for me. She can do anything—in fact, she can even spin gold out of straw."

Now, the king was very fond of gold—he could never have enough of it. So he took the girl back with him to his palace and led her to an empty room at the top of a tower. As she wondered what was going to happen, first a spinning wheel and a chair were carried into the room, and then a big pile of hay. "Sit down," said the king. "Before tomorrow I want all that straw spun into gold."

"Oh no," said the girl. "I can't make gold out of straw. That was only my father showing off."

The king took no notice. He banged the door behind him and locked it.

The girl could not think of what to do. She was almost in tears when she heard a key turning in the lock. The door opened; in stepped a little man. He looked very strange. "What's the matter with you?" he asked.

"I'm in great trouble," said the girl. "The king has told me to spin all this straw into gold and I don't know how to do it."

"But I do," said the little man. "What will you give me if I do it for you?"

The girl was so glad that she said at once, "My necklace."

The little man grabbed the necklace and put it in his pocket. Then he made the girl sit on the floor in the corner, while he settled himself at the spinning wheel.

The girl thought she had closed her eyes for only a second but when she opened them again, it was morning. There was a big pile of gold beside her. The little man had disappeared.

When the king came into the room, he laughed with pleasure.

"Now may I go home?" said the girl. "Not yet," replied the king. "Let's see whether you can make me some more gold."

So that evening, another pile of straw was brought. Again the door was locked, and again the little man appeared. "What will you give me this time?" he said.

"All I have is this ring on my finger," replied the girl tearfully.

The little man pulled the ring from her finger and put it on his own. As he started to spin, the girl again felt her eyes close. Although she meant to stay awake, she slept until it was morning. There was another pile of gold beside her.

When the king saw the gold, he wanted yet more. The girl pleaded with him to be allowed to go home. He told her that if she would spin for one more night, he would marry her.

On the third night, when the little man appeared, she told him she had nothing left to give him, but that the king had promised to marry her.

"In that case," said the little man, "I will take the first child you have when you are married."

The girl knew she had to agree and comforted herself by thinking there might never be a child. So the same thing happened as on the first two nights. The next morning, the king found an even bigger pile of gold and started planning the wedding without delay.

The girl was very happy when she became queen. She was happier still when her first baby was born. She had quite forgotten what the little man had said. But he had not; one day, he came and ordered the queen to give him her child.

The queen cried so much that the little man took pity on her. "I will make a bargain

with you," he said. "If within three days you can tell me what my name is, you can keep your baby."

The queen stopped crying, but lay awake all night thinking of all the names she knew. The next day she sent out messengers to every part of the kingdom to make lists of every name anyone had ever heard.

When the little man came again, she began by asking if his name was Tom, or Dick, or Harry—but he said "No" to all of them. He looked at the baby in her cradle and went away grinning.

The next day the queen tried longer names. "Is it Benjamin? Is it Zachariah? Is it Jonathan?"

But the little man smiled and said, "No, that's not my name."

Early on the third day, one of the messengers came to the queen and told her that on his travels, he had come upon a little house in the woods. In front of it burned a fire, and around the fire skipped a little man. This is what he was singing.

"Tomorrow what a feast I'll make.

I'll brew some beer and bake some cake;

Merrily I'll dance and sing

For next day will a princess bring.

Never will the queen proclaim

That Rumpelstiltskin is my name!"

The queen was so pleased when she heard this, that she thanked the messenger and gathered all her court together. Then she sat on her throne with the baby beside her. The little princess smiled and gurgled in her cradle, as if she knew her mother would never give her up.

Then in came the little man, skipping and chuckling at the thought that he had won the baby.

"Now tell me what my name is!" he shouted.

Very slowly the queen said, "Is it Jack?"

"No, your highness," said the little man triumphantly.

"Is it . . . Will?" asked the queen.

"No, it is not."

The queen paused and said quietly, "Could your name be Rumpelstiltskin?"

The little man shrieked. "It was a witch who told you that!" he cried.

He stamped his foot so hard it went right through the floor. He had to use both hands to pull it out. He slunk away while the courtiers laughed.

The queen lifted the princess in her arms and kissed her. "Goodbye, Mr. Rumpelstiltskin," she said. "We wish you a merry feast in your own company."

THE PRINCESS AND
THE PEA

THERE WAS ONCE A PRINCE who wanted a wife. But not just any girl would do—she had to be a real princess. So he set off around the world, visiting the royal families of all the kingdoms he could find. Every princess he met wanted to marry him, but not one of them lived up to his dream of what a princess should be.

When he had seen them all, the prince came home and felt very sad and lonely.

One night there was a flash of lightning in the sky, followed quickly by a crash of thunder and then down came the rain! It made so much noise that only the prince's father, the king, heard a knock at the palace door. When he opened it, there stood a girl who was very, very wet and shivering with cold. Her long hair was dripping down her back like rats' tails and her clothes clung to her. Her toes squished in her shoes as she stamped her feet, trying to get warm.

"Please let me in," she said. "I know the prince will be glad to see me, because I'm a real princess."

"Well, we'll soon find out," thought the queen to herself, as she hurried the girl to the fire to take off her wet clothes.

While the girl warmed herself, the queen went to make up the bed for her in the palace's guest room. First she looked in a kitchen cupboard for one tiny dried pea, and then she placed it carefully in the middle of the bare bedstead. Next, on top of the pea, she put the mattress, and another, and another—until there were twenty mattresses in the pile. Then she fetched twenty eiderdowns stuffed with the softest duck feathers and threw those up one by one on top of the mattresses. The girl was so tired that she

thought she would fall asleep the moment she closed her eyes.

Next morning, at breakfast, the queen asked, "And how did you sleep last night?" The girl frowned and replied, "I couldn't sleep at all. I think there must have been a stone in that bed because I am bruised all over."

Then everyone knew the girl was a real princess, because she had felt the pea even though it was covered by twenty mattresses and twenty eiderdowns. Only a real princess would have such sensitive skin.

So the prince had found his wife at last, and we may be sure they lived happily ever after. The pea was preserved in the royal museum, where one day you may find it, if it hasn't been stolen.

And this story, like the princess, was a real one.

BEAUTY AND
THE BEAST

THERE WAS ONCE A RICH MERCHANT who had six children—three sons and three daughters. He spent a lot of money hiring tutors to teach them at home, but his two eldest daughters wanted only to have a good time and would not do their lessons.

The youngest daughter was the prettiest of them all, so her father called her "Beauty"—which made her sisters very jealous. While they liked to spend all day playing and all night dancing, Beauty was content being with her father and reading her books.

Then came a day when there was no more money. The merchant told his children that they must move out of their fine town house and go to live in a small farm in the country, where they would all have to work. The father and his three sons tilled the fields and tended the cattle. Beauty got up at four o'clock every morning to clean the house, wash their clothes, and prepare all the meals for the family. At the end of the day, she would read her books and play her harpsichord. Her sisters did nothing but lie in bed and complain that they could no longer go dancing.

After a year, Beauty's father heard there might be some money owed to him in the town. Before he set off, his two eldest daughters begged him to bring them back new dresses, hats, and ribbons. "What would you like, Beauty?" asked her father. Beauty thought to herself that he might not have money to buy presents for them all. So she told him that the only thing she would like was one red rose—because no roses grew on the farm.

When the merchant reached the town, he found there was no fortune waiting for him. Very discouraged, he began his return journey home. As he rode through the

forest, it began to snow. The wind was so strong that he twice fell off his horse. Then he realized he was quite lost. Suddenly he spotted a light far ahead. As he came nearer, he saw that it came from a palace, where a light shone from every window. His horse made straight for an open stable door. Inside it, he found no other horses, but a manger full of hay and oats.

The front door of the palace also stood open, so the merchant stepped into the hall. First he dried himself at the fire, thinking that he would explain what had happened when the owner of the palace appeared. But nobody came. He waited until it was nearly midnight. By then, he was so tired and hungry. He ate the food that he found on a table laid for one, shut the front door, and went upstairs to bed.

When he awoke the next morning, he discovered that his wet clothes had been taken away and fresh garments hung in their place. He looked out of the window and saw that the snow had all gone. In the gardens outside, flowers bloomed.

Going downstairs to the hall, where he had eaten supper the night before, he smelt a jug of hot chocolate set on the table. "Some good fairy is looking after me," he said to himself.

On his way to collect his horse from the stable, he walked through the gardens he had seen from the window. Remembering Beauty's wish, he picked one red rose for her. Straightaway there was a thunderous crash, and before him stood a monstrous beast. "What an ungrateful wretch you are," growled the monster. "I have saved your life by giving you shelter in my palace. And how do you repay me? By stealing one of my roses, which are more precious to me than anything in the world. For this you will die!"

The merchant was terrified. "My Lord," he stuttered, "please forgive me. I took the rose not for myself but for one of my daughters."

"My name is not 'My Lord,'" interrupted the monster. "My name is Beast. I will forgive you—but on one condition. If one of your daughters is willing to take your place, then I will spare you."

So the merchant gave his word that he would return within three months, or send one of his daughters in his place—if only he could return home and see his children once more. Beast agreed. To the merchant's surprise, the Beast said he need not go back empty-handed. He should have a chest full of gold pieces.

On his arrival home, the merchant's eldest daughters were not pleased when he told his story and confessed that he had not brought the new dresses, hats, and ribbons, but only the red rose, for which he had to pay with his life. They turned on Beauty. "You wanted to be different by not asking for clothes as we did! Now see what you've done. You will be the death of our father and you're not even crying."

"Why should I?" answered Beauty. "I won't let my father die. The monster said he would take one of us instead. I shall happily go to Beast's palace and show him how much I love my father."

Then Beauty's brothers said no—they would go and kill the monster. Her father protested that it didn't matter if he died, since he was old and had only a few more years to live. But in the end, Beauty had her way and made her father let her follow him to Beast's palace.

When they said goodbye, Beauty's brothers wept but her sisters had to rub their eyes with onions to make them cry because they were glad to see her go. Their father had already given them the chest full of gold pieces. They knew that this would soon find them husbands.

Beauty and her father rode to the palace. As before, there in the hall was the table covered with succulent dishes—this time laid with two places. The merchant didn't feel like eating, but Beauty tasted a little. When she had finished, the monster appeared so suddenly that she was very frightened. Beast asked her if she had come willingly. When she said yes, he thanked her. Then the Beast told her father to leave the palace the next day and never come back.

Beauty's father hated leaving her, but she remained cheerful until he was gone. Then she cried and cried, because she was sure that the monster intended to eat her that night. After a time, she decided she'd cried enough and might as well explore the palace while she could. Very soon she came to a door marked "Beauty's Apartment" and this led to a suite of rooms including a library, in which stood a harpsichord. "Someone must be expecting me to use these rooms for longer than one day," she thought. "Perhaps Beast doesn't want me to die just yet." So she took down a book from the library shelves. On the first page she read:

"Welcome Beauty, banish fear,

You are queen and mistress here:

Speak your wishes, speak your will,

Swift obedience meets them still."

"Oh," said she. "What I wish most is to see my dear father." No sooner had she said this than she saw in a looking glass her father reaching home, his face still wet with tears.

That evening when she was about to sit down to supper, the monster appeared. She was again very frightened. "Why are you so afraid?" he said. "Am I so ugly?"

"Yes," answered Beauty. "I cannot tell a lie. But I do believe you have a generous nature."

"So I have," said the monster. "But I am ugly and I think I'm a bit stupid."

"It is no shame to think so," answered Beauty. "Only a fool is not aware of his foolishness. I'd rather have you as you are than a man who hides his nasty nature behind a handsome face."

By now, Beauty had stopped being frightened of the monster and ate all her supper. Beast watched her and then said, "Beauty, will you be my wife?"

At this she almost fainted and was afraid he would be angry if she refused. At last she said, "No, Beast." With a great sigh that echoed through the palace, he left her.

The next evening, he came again and asked her the same question. He did this for three months. Slowly Beauty began to look forward to his coming, because he talked to her with good common sense, if not wit. One day, he said that, though he knew she would never marry him, he hoped she would never leave him. Beauty answered that she could only promise this if he would let her see her father once more. In her looking glass, she had seen that her sisters were both married and her brothers had gone to join the army, so her father was quite alone.

"You shall be with him tomorrow," said Beast. "Promise to come back in a week: when you are ready, just put your ring on the table before you go to bed."

Beauty woke up the next morning in her father's house. He was overjoyed to see her. The sisters came to visit but were even more jealous than before, when she told them how happy she was in Beast's palace. Both the sisters were disappointed in their husbands—one was handsome but so selfish he thought only about himself, the other was clever and witty but was always making jokes about his wife.

The sisters wickedly decided to persuade Beauty to stay for more than a week. Then the monster would be so angry with her for breaking her promise that he would devour her the moment she returned to the palace. So they wept real tears when the week ended. She agreed to stay longer. After three more days, Beauty woke in the night and felt miserable at what she had done. "I have been very unkind to Beast," she thought. "It's not his fault he is so ugly. He is thoughtful and generous, and I should marry him. I will be happier with him than my sisters are with their husbands."

So she put her ring on the table. The next morning she was back in the monster's palace. At supper time she waited to see Beast again but he did not come. Then she ran all through the palace looking for him and out into the gardens, where she found him stretched out on the grass, apparently dead. She fetched some water to pour over his face, whereupon Beast opened his eyes and said, "You forgot your promise to come back. But now that I have seen you again, I can die happy."

"Oh no," said Beauty. "You must not die. You must live to be my husband. I thought we could only be friends. But the grief that I felt when I believed you were dead has convinced me that I cannot live without you."

At that moment, the sound of joyful music came from the palace and fireworks sparkled in the sky. Beauty looked around and when she turned back the monster had gone. Kneeling at her feet was a young man.

"Where is my beloved Beast?" asked Beauty.

"You see him here," said the young man. "A wicked fairy has had me under a spell—making me look ugly and appear stupid. You have broken the spell by agreeing to marry me. Only you could see beyond my ugliness to my good nature. Now, in return, I can offer you a crown, for I am a prince and shall one day become king."

So the prince led Beauty back to the palace, where she found her father and the prince's whole family, who had been transported there by magic. Soon the prince and Beauty were married in his own kingdom and their happiness was complete.

THE END